Cornelius Black

# The Pathology of Tuberculous Bone

Anatiposi

**Cornelius Black**

# The Pathology of Tuberculous Bone

Reprint of the original.

1st Edition 2023 | ISBN: 978-3-38230-534-5

Anatiposi Verlag is an imprint of Outlook Verlagsgesellschaft mbH.

Verlag (Publisher): Outlook Verlag GmbH, Zeilweg 44, 60439 Frankfurt, Deutschland
Vertretungsberechtigt (Authorized to represent): E. Roepke, Zeilweg 44, 60439 Frankfurt, Deutschland
Druck (Print): Books on Demand GmbH, In de Tarpen 42, 22848 Norderstedt, Deutschland

# THE PATHOLOGY

OF

# TUBERCULOUS BONE.

By CORNELIUS BLACK, M.D., Lond.,

FELLOW OF THE ROYAL COLLEGE OF SURGEONS OF ENGLAND,

CORRESPONDING FELLOW OF THE IMPERIAL SOCIETY OF PHYSICIANS OF VIENNA,

MEMBER OF THE PATHOLOGICAL SOCIETY OF LONDON,

ETC., ETC., ETC.

EDINBURGH:

SUTHERLAND AND KNOX, 60, SOUTH BRIDGE.

MDCCCLIX.

# THE PATHOLOGY

OF

# TUBERCULOUS BONE.

BONE, like most other tissues of the body, is subject to various diseases, amongst which tuberculosis occupies a prominent position. This disease, when once it has invaded the bony texture, is perhaps as little controllable as tuberculosis of any other structure of the body. Its frequent occurrence during the epochs of childhood, boyhood, and adolescence—the ravages which it makes with the integrity of joints—and the maiming which necessarily attends any operative procedure for its removal, claim for it a more than ordinary attention on the part of the pathologist. I say, on the part of the pathologist, rather than on the part of the mere practical surgeon; because treatment, to be pursued upon correct principles, and with that probability of success which attends real knowledge, must ever be based upon a true pathology of the disease to which it is applied. The true pathology of disease not only embraces a correct knowledge of the morbific changes which take place in a part, but it predicates a knowledge of the anatomical structure and physiology of the tissue in which such changes occur.

Hence, anatomy and physiology are the scientific bases of pathology; whilst the latter, in conjunction with a knowledge of the therapeutical action of remedies, constitutes the rational basis of the treatment of disease. In tracing, in accordance with these views, the pathological changes of tuberculosis of bone, it will be necessary, for the proper appreciation of these changes, to premise an account of the minute anatomy of that structure in its healthy condition. As, however, tuberculosis of bone is, from the probable peculiarities of position, texture, circulation, and growth, limited to the cancellous portions of that structure, a detail of the minute anatomy of the latter only is requisite for the perfect understanding of the pathological data which I am about to introduce.

On placing a thin section, properly prepared for observation, of the extremities of long bones, or of the substance of any of the short bones, as those of the carpus or tarsus, in the microscope, it is seen to consist of a number of spaces, bounded by plates of bony substance, in which latter certain small bodies, more or less opaque, are situated. These components are named respectively cancelli—bony partitions, osseous lamellæ, or cancellous walls—and lacunæ.

The cancelli are the cells or vacuities of bone, which give to that structure, on a superficial inspection, a spongy, honey-combed, or worm-eaten appearance. They are, generally, regularly or irregularly ovoid, now and then almost spherical, communicate freely with each other, and are lined by a fine vascular membrane, which, in bones with a medullary cavity, is, on the one hand, continuous with the vascular membrane which lines that cavity, and, on the other, with the periosteum through the numerous minute openings, or vascular bony canals, seen on the surface of the expanded extremities of long bones.

In order to determine accurately their respective diameters in different specimens of cancellous bone, the microscope was so arranged that the 1-100ths of an inch on the stage micrometer were each enlarged to such a degree, that the image thrown by a camera upon a piece of paper was exactly equal to an inch. The micrometer having been removed, portions of bone were substituted, and these were, therefore, magnified 100 diameters. The images of the different cancelli thus thrown down, having been traced, their diameters were accurately measured by compasses, so many 1-10ths of an inch on the drawing representing as many 1-1000ths of an inch in the real size of the specimen. By this means, which is not only the readiest, but also the most correct, method of measuring objects to which it can be applied, the following results, as to the mean diameters of the cancelli, were obtained :—

MEAN DIAMETERS OF CANCELLI OF HEALTHY BONE.

|  | Long Diameter. | Short Diameter. |
|---|---|---|
| A | $9\frac{1}{2}$ | 9 |
| B | 18 | 15 |
| C | $12\frac{1}{2}$ | 7 |
| D | 12 | 7 |
| E | 7 | $3\frac{1}{2}$ |
| F | 15 | 10 |
| G | $16\frac{1}{2}$ | 14 |
| H | 21 | 12 |
| I | 10 | 6 |
| K | 22 | 19 |
|  | $143\frac{1}{2}$ | $102\frac{1}{2}$ |
| Mean average | $\frac{14.36}{1000}$ths inch. | $\frac{10.26}{1000}$ths inch. |

It will hereafter be shown, that these diameters are decidedly and manifestly increased by the progress of tuberculous disease in the osseous tissue. In the meantime, however, it must be remarked, that the cancelli are, in their healthy condition, more or less occupied by large, delicate fat-cells, in which, in many instances, the stearine and margarine are seen to have crystallised. By boiling, for a short time, a section of cancellous bone in æther or alcohol, the fatty contents of the cancelli are dissolved, and these, by subsequent evaporation, admit of accurate determination. A solution of potash produces a similar effect, in addition to which, numerous granules and irregular patches of the lining membrane of the cancelli are detached, and freely interspersed amongst the oil-globules under observation. The vascular membrane which lines the cancelli is of great tenuity, and consists of a basement structure surmounted by a layer of flattened cells of somewhat irregular figure. Beneath this structure the vessels of the bone constitute a beautiful network, which, in long bones, is formed by the anastomoses of the vessels of the medullary cavity extended outwards, with the vessels of the periosteum passing inwards; and, in those bones which have no such medullary cavity, by the latter vessels in their course throughout the entire substance of such bones. It will thus be seen how intimate is the vascular connection between the exterior and interior parts of bone, and how readily injury applied to the former may affect the integrity of the latter of this structure. In the healthy condition of bone, the vascular membrane of the cancelli, and also of the medullary cavity, manifests but little sensibility; but, in a state of disease, it is frequently the seat of exquisite suffering.

To view the minute structure of the osseous lamellæ, or bony partitions of the cancelli, a section of bone, after having been brought, by the process of rubbing and polishing, into the required thinness for microscopic observation, may be boiled, for a few minutes, in æther or alcohol, for the purpose of removing the fatty contents of the cancelli. In this condition, the general microscopic aspect of the lamellæ presents the appearance of multitudes of granules thickly set in an unequally shaded, homogeneous matrix, interspersed throughout with numerous lacunæ, and, here and there, with fibres either isolated, in parallel course with others, or grouped into bands of a somewhat wavy disposition.

The granular appearance in question is due to the presence of the ultimate particles of bone, which may be separated from their matrix by incineration, by prolonged boiling in a Papin's digester, or by digestion in boiling liquor potassæ. Thus isolated, they are calcareous in their composition, oval, oblong, or irregularly angular in their figure, and measure from 1-5700th to 1-13,000th of an inch in their longest diameter.

## FIGURE I.

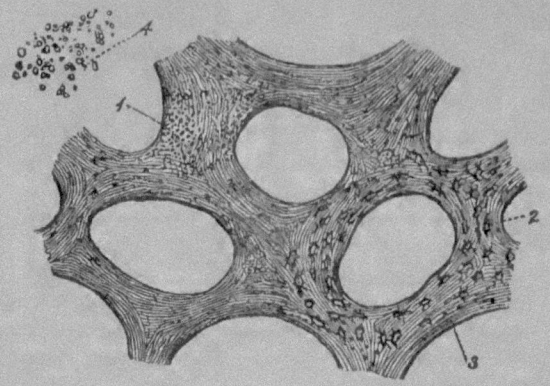

Fig. I.—1. Granular appearance of cancellous bone after being boiled in æther.
2. Lacunæ of cancellous bone.
3. Fibrous tissue of cancellous bone.
4. Ultimate earthy particles of bone.

The matrix in which the ultimate earthy particles of bone are set, although, when viewed under the above conditions, or after the subsequent addition of liquor potassæ, or of the spirit of turpentine, presents a homogeneous appearance, yet it is in reality *fibro-gelatinous* in its intimate structure. This character is best shown by digesting a section of bone in a mixture of one part of hydrochloric acid and ten parts of water until the earthy salts have been dissolved, and by subsequently submitting a fine shred of the fibro-gelatinous matrix to microscopic observation. It will now be seen that each cancellus is surrounded by a flat band of fibres, varying from 1-400th to 1-1000th of an inch in breadth, which of itself, as it were, defines the boundary of the cancellus, and which consists of fibrillæ from 1-15,000th to 1-20,000th of an inch in diameter. These fibrillæ are somewhat wavy in their disposition, and are, in every respect, similar to those of the white fibrous tissue. Between these fibrous bands, circumscribing the cancelli, numerous other fibres, not grouped into bands, but in an isolated condition, and at more or less regular intervals, decussate each other at acute angles. These also manifest the appearance of the white fibrous tissue. But amongst them are frequently seen other fibres running, at intervals of 1-1000th of an inch, in a parallel direction with the long diameter of the adjacent cancelli, giving off, here and there, a branch at an acute angle, and presenting, both in their diameter and general arrangement, the character of the yellow elastic fibrous tissue. All these fibres, now enumerated, are imbedded in a hyaline substance, with which they constitute the fibro-gelatinous matrix of cancellous bone.

FIGURE II.

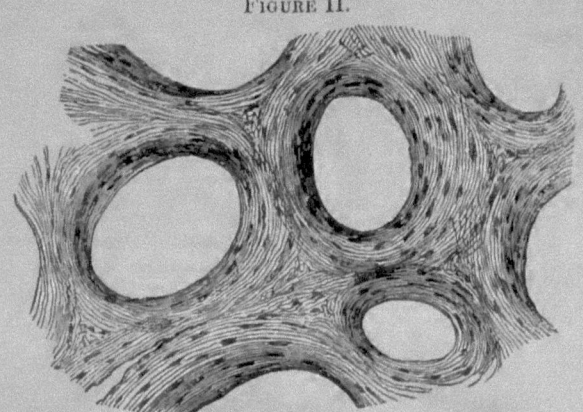

Fig. II. Fibrous tissue of cancellous bone. Drawn under the Camera Lucida, by that able artist, Mr Tuffen West, of London.

This substance, in its calcified state, constitutes the osseous walls of the cancelli, which, in healthy bone, have the following diameters, as determined by mean measurement.

MEAN DIAMETERS OF THE OSSEOUS WALLS OF HEALTHY CANCELLOUS BONE.

| | | |
|---|---|---|
| $a$ | . . | 10 |
| $b$ | . . | 9 |
| $c$ | . . | 6 |
| $d$ | . . | $9\frac{1}{2}$ |
| $e$ | . . | $7\frac{1}{2}$ |
| $f$ | . . | 12 |
| $g$ | . . | 9 |
| $h$ | . . | 6 |
| $i$ | . . | 6 |
| $j$ | . . | 4 |
| $k$ | . . | 12 |
| $l$ | . . | 10 |
| $m$ | . . | 13 |
| $n$ | . . | 8 |
| $o$ | . . | 12 |
| $p$ | . . | 10 |
| $q$ | . . | 12 |
| $r$ | . . | 5 |
| $s$ | . . | 9 |
| $t$ | . . | 9 |
| | | ——— |
| | | 179 |

Mean average $\frac{8.1.0}{1000}$ths inch.

It will, hereafter, be shown, that these diameters are materially diminished by the disintegration of the osseous walls of the cancelli during the third stage of tuberculosis of bone. At present, however, it is sufficient to indicate that fact, and to pass to the remark, that where several cancelli of healthy bone approach one point from different directions, a quadrangular space of bone is mapped out, the diameter of which is often twice that of the osseous lamellæ interposed between adjacent cancelli.

If a fine section of cancellous bone, from which the fat has been previously abstracted, be submitted to microscopic examination, numerous bodies, opaque in their appearance, will be seen in linear arrangement throughout the substance of each osseous lamella. These are the lacunæ, which, in their figure, are either lenticular, oblong, irregularly ovate, or irregularly stellate. The first two forms represent the lacunæ situated in the osseous lamellæ between adjacent cancelli, the mean measurements of which gave the following diameters:—

FIGURE III.

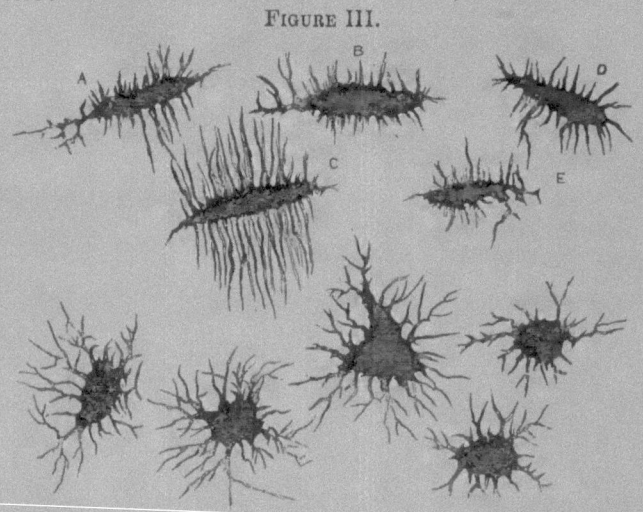

Fig. III.—Lacunæ of bone—Magnified 500 diameters.

| | Long Diameter. | Short Diameter. |
|---|---|---|
| A | $\frac{1}{588}$th inch. | $\frac{1}{4000}$th inch. |
| B | $\frac{1}{666}$th ,, | $\frac{1}{2857}$th ,, |
| C | $\frac{1}{769}$th ,, | $\frac{1}{5000}$th ,, |
| D | $\frac{1}{1000}$th ,, | $\frac{1}{2000}$th ,, |
| E | $\frac{1}{1250}$th ,, | $\frac{1}{3333}$th ,, |
| Mean average | $\frac{1}{864}$th ,, | $\frac{1}{3438}$th ,, |

The last two mentioned forms of lacunæ are most frequently observed in the quadrangular islets of bone before named. These vary in length from 1-1000th to 1-2000th of an inch, and in breadth from 1-1429th to 1-2000th of an inch. In the arrangement of the lacunæ, their long diameter is invariably directed towards the adjacent cancellus. From their sides minute tubes or pores, termed canaliculi, proceed. These, in the series of lacunæ lying nearest to a cancellus, communicate, on the one hand, with the latter, and, on the other, with the canaliculi of the lacunæ next in order from the cancellus. They proceed nearly in straight lines, and give off very few branches; whilst those of the lacunæ situated in the quadrangular islets of bone before described, are of an arborescent character, branching repeatedly and dichotomously, thus resembling a bush in miniature. They vary in diameter from 1-5000th of an inch at their origin, to 1-15,000th or 1-20,000th of an inch in their finer ramifications; whilst the diameter of the most minute of their branches is even stated not to exceed the 1-40,000th or the 1-60,000th of an inch. By this arrangement of the lacunæ, canaliculi, and their branches throughout the whole breadth of the osseous lamella, the latter is so channeled, that the nutritive blastema of the blood is readily conveyed to every part of the osseous tissue.

It is, however, clear from the extreme minuteness of the canaliculi and their branches, that the red globules of the blood cannot pass through them, and that they, therefore, only convey the unorganised portion of that fluid.

Viewed in a dry section of bone, both the lacunæ and their canaliculi appear as opaque bodies. This opacity, however, does not, as it would at first sight appear, depend on the presence of a substance deposited in their cavities and channels respectively; for, on the addition of a small quantity of the spirit of turpentine to the section under observation, this fluid is seen to enter the lacunæ and to render them at once transparent; and afterwards, to make its way into the canaliculi, which are thereby rendered as so many transparent lines. Again, after a section of bone has had its calcareous matter removed by a dilute mineral acid, the lacunæ are seen as so many granular cells, the cavities of which are empty; whilst their granules or nuclei stand prominently forth, in number from three to seven. The addition now of a solution of potash to such a preparation, dissolves entirely, or nearly so, the cell-walls, and thus destroys the organic matrix of the lacunæ.

I shall, however, hereafter show, that although, in healthy bone, the lacunæ are, in a great measure, unoccupied by deposit, yet in the tuberculous condition of that structure, they are frequently *stuffed* with an exudation, which plays an important part in the pathological changes which subsequently occur.

The following is the composition of healthy cancellous bone, as determined by chemical analysis of the subjoined specimens :—

Composition of condyles of healthy femur in young adult male.

| Organic Matter. | 1st Specimen. | 2d Specimen. | 3d Specimen. |
|---|---|---|---|
| Cartilage and vessels, | 13·85 | 14·13 | 16·30 |
| Fat, | 49·05 | 58·00 | 48·00 |
| **Inorganic Matter.** | | | |
| Phosphate of lime with fluoride (?) of calcium, | 33·45 | 23·88 | 32·20 |
| Carbonate of lime, | 2·70 | 3·07 | 2·70 |
| Phosphate of magnesia, | ·37 | ·45 | ·30 |
| Soluble salts, | ·58 | ·47 | ·50 |
| | 100·00 | 100·00 | 100·00 |

## Composition of the head of healthy tibia in young adult male.

| Organic Matter. | 1st Specimen. | 2d Specimen. | 3d Specimen. |
|---|---|---|---|
| Cartilage and vessels, | 22·18 | 20·25 | 21·94 |
| Fat, | 44·60 | 48·14 | 45·98 |
| **Inorganic Matter.** | | | |
| Phosphate of lime with fluoride (?) of calcium, | 29·07 | 27·65 | 28·05 |
| Carbonate of lime, | 3·00 | 2·87 | 2·93 |
| Phosphate of magnesia, | ·38 | ·35 | ·36 |
| Soluble salts, | ·77 | ·74 | ·74 |
| | 100·00 | 100·00 | 100·00 |

## Composition of healthy astragalus in young adult male.

| Organic Matter. | | | |
|---|---|---|---|
| Cartilage and vessels, | 24·08 | 26·59 | 25.98 |
| Fat, | 38·46 | 32·83 | 35·39 |
| **Inorganic Matter.** | | | |
| Phosphate of lime with fluoride (?) of calcium, | 32·19 | 35·26 | 33·44 |
| Carbonate of lime, | 4·04 | 4·03 | 3·98 |
| Phosphate of magnesia, | ·50 | ·55 | ·52 |
| Soluble salts, | ·73 | ·74 | ·69 |
| | 100·00 | 100·00 | 100·00 |

## Composition of healthy os calcis in young adult male.

| Organic Matter. | | | |
|---|---|---|---|
| Cartilage and vessels, | 26·59 | 17·81 | 22·44 |
| Fat, | 39·02 | 54·16 | 45·69 |
| **Inorganic Matter.** | | | |
| Phosphate of lime and fluoride (?) of calcium, | 30·00 | 23·87 | 27·58 |
| Carbonate of lime, | 3·05 | 2·93 | 3·00 |
| Phosphate of magnesia, | ·37 | ·30 | ·42 |
| Soluble salts, | ·97 | ·93 | ·87 |
| | 100·00 | 100·00 | 100·00 |

Having thus described the microscopic anatomy and chemical composition of healthy cancellous bone, it will be easy to understand the pathological changes which result from tuberculosis of that structure. This affection, like tuberculosis of the lungs, is a disease of the earlier epochs of life, and presents three pathological stages for consideration—namely,

    I. The stage of active congestion or local predisposition.

    II. The stage of exudation.

    III. The stage of germination and ulceration.

### STAGE OF ACTIVE CONGESTION.

The opportunities which are offered to the pathologist of submitting to microscopic examination the first stage of tuberculosis of bone, never, except by accident, occurs whilst the disease is limited to that stage alone. It is when the ravages of disease in the bony tissue, or in an adjacent joint, or in both, have demanded operative interference, that such opportunities arise; but fortunately in such instances, as in tuberculosis of the lungs, all the stages of the disease are observable in the same specimen.

To the unaided sight, the first stage of tuberculosis of bone is revealed by an injected appearance of the osseous tissue, which is of a deep red colour, and which seems to be more soddened with fluid than bone of a healthy character. Here and there, over the surface of the simply injected portions of bone, are small coagula of blood, which lie within the cavity of one or more cancelli, which are consequently moulded to their figure, and which adhere more or less closely to their walls.

Microscopically examined, a properly prepared section of such bone exhibits the network of capillaries, lying immediately beneath the lining membrane of the cancelli, inordinately distended with blood. At some points this distension is so great, that the inter-capillary spaces are almost obliterated by the lateral encroachment of enlarged vessels; whilst, at other points, the distension is less, and the inter-capillary spaces are consequently more apparent. Again, at various points of the vascular network of the cancelli, the capillaries are irregularly distended, and apparently on the point of bursting; whilst, at other points, they have already yielded to the pressure upon their walls, and extravasation of blood into the corresponding cancelli has taken place. In those cases which run a rapid course, the vascular injection is pretty equal throughout the affected osseous tissue; but, in those of slower progress, there are not unfrequently islets of bone mapped out, as it were, in deeper tint and coloration than the intervening portions, thus giving to the general appearance a more or less variegated hue. In the short bones, the vessels passing through the periosteum are likewise injected; and this membrane itself has in consequence acquired a puffy, rosy appearance. In the extremities of long bones not only are the periosteal vessels engorged, but, in those cases in which active congestion pervades the whole extent of such extremities, the vessels distributed on the medullary membrane, at the point of continuation of the latter with that of the cancelli, are similarly involved.

Now, the symptoms to which this pathological condition gives rise, are—a sensation of aching, weight, or soreness in the affected bone—increased heat—puffiness of the superjacent soft parts, with more or less vascular injection—some tenderness on pressure—restricted motion of the neighbouring joint, with a sense of pain and stiffness on attempted movement—and, to a greater or less extent, sympathetic disturbance in the general system.

In the extremities of long bones this condition may be either primary or secondary. If the former, its tendency, when uncontrolled, is to extend to the neighbouring joint, which swells, becomes painful, stiff, and more or less crippled in its movements. The natural depressions around the joint fill up, sometimes in the course of a day or two ; at other times, not until the lapse of a week or longer. The shorter the period in this respect, the greater the tenderness and heat of the affected part, and the more the system sympathises with the local affection. Hence, all shades of intensity of the local symptoms occur in this stage—from those which indicate the least departure from the natural condition, to those which express the approaching development of acute inflammation.

When tuberculosis of bone is secondary, it is preceded by a similar pathological condition of the synovial membrane and cartilages of the adjacent joint, which has probably existed for months, or even for one or two years, and which has, in many cases, already passed into the ulcerative stage at the time the osseous tissue first becomes involved. In the extremities of long bones the secondary form of the disease is the more frequent, and it occurs as a natural consequence of the progressive extension of tuberculosis from the tissues of the neighbouring joint. But in the primary form it is generally the result of direct injury applied to the bone itself; and to this point the symptoms of pain, tenderness, increased heat, and sensation of weight are, for an indefinite period, confined.

In illustration of the above stage of the primary form of tuberculosis of bone, it will be sufficient to quote the following examples :—

CASE I.—C. G., a boy aged 7 years, of nervous temperament, with light hair and eyes, fine, delicate skin, and of slender build, accidentally fell whilst at play, in the early part of March 1856. In the fall the head of the right tibia came into contact with a loose stone, from which he experienced sharp pain for a few minutes. This in a great measure subsided, and he resumed his play ; nevertheless, he continued his exertions with an evident degree of pain. On the following day, he was observed to favour the affected limb in both standing and walking ; but his parents, attributing the symptoms to the injury received on the previous day, viewed them with no alarm, and, in the expectation that a few days would remove them, did as yet nothing in the case. From day to day, however, the symptoms of pain and lameness increased, and, on the fifth after the accident, I saw him.

Over the head of the tibia the integuments were puffed, somewhat injected with blood, and hotter than natural. The inner side of the knee-joint was rounded, and the knee itself somewhat flexed. From the tubercle of the tibia backwards along the inner margin of its head, pressure aggravated a fixed pain, which was also increased on flexing and extending the knee-joint. There was a sensation of constant aching over the head of the tibia, and sometimes along the shaft of this bone, which was increased by hanging the limb down, and aggravated at night. The outer side of the joint was natural in appearance, and gave no evidence of pain on firm pressure over the head of the fibula and the external condyle of the femur. The general system manifested some disturbance in a slight acceleration of pulse, furred tongue, slight thirst, deficient appetite, occasionally increased heat of skin, and unusual wakefulness.

The treatment was commenced by the application of four leeches to the head of the tibia, followed by almost constant fomentations of hot poppy-and-camomile decoction, and, in the absence of fomentations, by enveloping the knee-joint in a hot bran poultice. The limb was laid at perfect rest upon a

Liston's splint, and the greatest quietude of the part was rigidly maintained. A saline aperient was administered, and was followed by the regular exhibition of small doses of mercury and chalk, Dover's powder, acetate of ammonia, and the spirit of nitrous æther, together, at the very outset, with a minute proportion of antimony. The diet was restricted to milk, rice, and similar food.

In ten days the local symptoms had subsided, and little more than a mere feebleness of the limb remained. It was, however, evident that the affected part was as yet unfit to bear the weight of the body; therefore, to prevent any attempt to use it, the limb was encased in thin pasteboard splints and starched bandages, and the patient put upon crutches. For five weeks absolute quietude of the limb was thus insured, and the patient in consequence made a perfect recovery.

CASE II.—M. C., a girl, aged 11 years, of nervo-sanguineous temperament, with fair complexion, light hair and eyes, of symmetrical figure, and of great vivacity, with constitution hereditarily predisposed to tuberculosis, fell whilst dancing, and struck with some degree of force the inner side of the right knee upon the floor. The fall caused her at the time pain in the part struck; but nothing was then done in regard to it. Three days afterwards a certain degree of awkwardness and apparent lameness attracted the attention of her parents, by whom I was immediately called to the case. It was observed that the patient, when standing, favoured the affected part, by slightly advancing the right leg, and by somewhat flexing the corresponding knee-joint. Her gait was marked by a perceptible halt, and progression was evidently accompanied by pain. On examination, there was found a fulness of the integuments over the head of the tibia, with a manifest increase of heat, but no redness of the skin.

Two inches to the inner side of the anterior tuberosity of the tibia, and about an inch below the articulating surface of that bone, was the chief seat of uneasiness. From this point a sensation of aching extended along the shaft of the bone, which was variable in its character during the day, but which was generally worse at night. Here pressure aggravated the uneasiness, which was likewise increased by any motion of the knee-joint. Gentle percussion over the remaining portion of the head of the tibia elicited expressions of more or less pain; but the same method of examination, applied to the head of the fibula and to the external condyle of the femur, gave no uneasiness whatever. During the last two nights, the patient, startled by dreams of some impending danger, had frequently and suddenly risen from sleep with expressions of considerable alarm. This condition of the nervous system was further manifested, during the waking state, by irritability of temper, by failing appetite, and by other symptoms of increasing disturbance in the general system.

From the first moment of treatment, the affected limb was laid at *perfect rest*, and not a single attempt to move it was permitted. The head of the tibia was depleted by leeches, and subsequently soothed by the above-mentioned anodyne fomentation, in conjunction with poultices of scalded bran sufficiently large to envelope the whole of the knee-joint. A brisk aperient was given, and the case was subsequently treated with alterative doses of mercury and chalk, in conjunction with Dover's powder, acetate of ammonia, and other remedies similar to Case I. The diet consisted of milk and the different farinacea. After active congestion had, by these means, been relieved, the limb was encased in pasteboard splints and starched bandages, and kept in complete rest for three weeks longer, at the end of which time all trace of disease had disappeared.

In contrast with the effects of treatment in the above cases is the following:—

CASE III.—W. H., a boy aged 7 years, of sanguineo-lymphatic temperament, with fair and rosy complexion, and more than ordinary rotundity of body, was observed by his parents to halt somewhat in his walk, and to favour the left lower extremity. On inquiry, he complained of pain over the head of the tibia; but he could not refer it to any injury. He, however, remembered that a few days before, he had, whilst playing, received a blow somewhere about the knee, which caused him pain for a short time. For several days after detecting his lameness, his parents, regarding the affection as the natural result of the blow, and expecting that a short time would set the matter right, did nothing in the case. The lameness, however, continued to increase from day to day, and at length I saw him.

The integuments over the inner side of the knee-joint, but particularly over the head of the tibia, were now swollen, hot, and painful on pressure. Percussion over the head of the tibia gave considerable pain at the time, which was followed by a sensation of aching in the part percussed, as also along the shaft of the bone. Frequently, during the night, the head and shaft of the tibia, but particularly the former, were the seat of a gnawing sensation which prevented sleep. The outer side of the knee-joint was natural in appearance and free from pain. The knee itself was bent, so that the toes and part of the plantar surface only rested upon the ground. Any attempt to place the heel upon the ground produced pain in and behind the knee. The patient had, within the last few days, lost appetite, had thirst, and was fretful and irritable. The pulse was slightly accelerated, the tongue thinly covered with a dirty white fur, the skin hotter than natural, the urine scanty and highly coloured, but depositing no sediment, and the bowels were torpid.

The treatment consisted, as before, of *perfect rest* of the part, local depletion by leeches, anodyne fomentations and poultices, a brisk aperient at the outset, followed by the use of mercurial alteratives, alkalies, and Dover's powder, and by a milk and farinaceous diet. In a fortnight from the commencement of this treatment, all active symptoms had subsided in the affected part, and the general system had, to a certain extent, recovered its usual tone. The limb was now encased in splints and starched bandages, with the view of maintaining, for several weeks longer, absolute quietude of the joint. This restriction was impatiently borne but for a fortnight, after which the mother, yielding to the urgent entreaties of her child, and fancying herself that further confinement was unnecessary, stripped off the appliances, and permitted the patient at once to join his companions in their sport. For two or three weeks recovery appeared to be complete—neither pain, lameness, nor any distortion of the joint being present. By and by, however, a slight halting in the gait, a favouring of the affected limb whilst standing, and some degree of flexure of the knee-joint, were observed. Pain, swelling, and increased heat of the integuments over the inner side of the knee returned; but the general health remained as yet unaffected. The case was now, as to the local affection, in precisely the same condition as when I first saw it. Absolute rest, the great essential element in the treatment of such a case, was now stoutly refused by the parents, on the ground that the patient could not use crutches, and that "confinement would injure his health." Not being able to overcome the prejudices of both parents and child in this respect, I lost sight of the case. Six months afterwards I was again called to the patient, who had now sustained a fracture of the left humerus. On examining the knee, I found considerable extension of the disease. Exudation had taken place beneath the periosteum and within the head of the tibia, which was consequently greatly enlarged. This part was the seat of constant uneasiness, and of every sensation from a mere aching to that of a deep gnawing pain. Percussion, motion of the knee, or hanging the limb down, aggravated the local uneasiness. The synovial membrane of the knee-joint had become implicated, the knee itself was permanently flexed, the hamstring tendons were rigid and prominent, and the toes only rested upon the ground during progression. As the case was being allowed to take its course, it is certain that it will ultimately compromise the safety of the limb.

The indications of treatment in the first stage of tuberculosis of bone are :—

I. To remove active congestion.

II. To prevent its recurrence.

In fulfilling the former indication, local depletion is of the very first importance. It directly abstracts blood from the vessels passing through the periosteum to the substance of the bone, and, by thus relieving their tension and diminishing the supply to the capillaries of the vascular membrane of the cancelli, it favours the return of both the former and latter vessels to a natural condition of caliber and contractility. As the circulation through bone is less influenced by the heart's action than that of any other part, active congestion of this tissue is slower in its occurrence, and is of longer duration, than in any other structure of the body. Hence, some days may elapse from the commencement of active congestion to the second stage, or that of exudation. In proportion to the duration of this interval is the benefit to be derived from local depletion. In every case, and particularly in every instance in which active congestion is as yet confined to the osseous tissue, local depletion is the first step imperatively demanded in a proper attempt to restore the healthy condition of the part. It should be practised daily until the different sensations of uneasiness, aching, or gnawing, or of pain on manipulation, have, in a great measure, passed away.

With this must be conjoined *absolute rest* of the affected part, as motion of the latter would maintain the very condition which local depletion is intended to relieve. The affected part ought, therefore, to be laid at perfect rest ; and as, by the hanging down of a diseased limb, increased uneasiness shows the injurious effects of gravity, this must be removed either by the recumbent position, or by placing the diseased structure on a level with the rest part of the body. As an adjunct to this treatment, anodyne fomentations and poultices, by soothing the irritated nerves of the part, and by favouring congestion of the vessels of the skin to the relief of those of the osseous tissue itself, are of great value in such cases. Where, too, the general system sympathises with the local disturbance, occasional aperients, followed by the use of mercury with chalk, Dover's powder, Jacob's powder, tartar emetic, and the alkalies separately or combined, to allay local and general excitement, to promote diaphoresis, and to correct the different secretions, are of essential service, and ought not to be omitted. In the matter of diet, it is evident that active local congestion is incompatible with a stimulating food. Hence, milk and the different farinacea are almost the only articles which the patient ought, at this stage, to be allowed.

To compass the second indication, it is absolutely necessary, after active congestion has been removed, that the patient should not use the previously affected part too soon. Experience shows, and Case III. is particularly instructive in this respect, that after congestion has been removed, at least so far as we are able to determine, a certain proneness to relapse exists in the previously affected bone, and that, for some time after apparent recovery, motion of the part re-excites the disease in all its original intensity. Better, therefore, to maintain a tedious, and, in the opinion of the patient, an unnecessary quietude of the part, than permit it to be used a single day too soon. This may be done, in the case of the head of the tibia, either by the application of lateral thin pasteboard splints, supported by starched bandages from the toes to the upper part of the thigh, or by applying a rigid splint, properly padded, from the middle of the posterior part of the thigh to the lower border of the calf, and by supporting this with starched bandages enveloping the whole limb. By the latter method, which is often the preferable one, the motions of the knee-joint are effectually restrained, and the affected part is not subjected to undue pressure; whilst, in both instances, the aid of crutches enables the patient to take exercise during the process of cure.

If the ankle-joint or bones of the tarsus are the seat of disease, the starched bandages are the only necessary appliances after the previous treatment has been carried sufficiently far. The foot, in such cases, and, indeed, in all cases involving any portion of the lower extremity, must be supported by a sling, which should pass round the neck, and be sufficiently long to bear the sole one or two inches from the ground during progression. On no account whatever is the patient to bear the *least weight* on the affected limb; but, on the contrary, every act of progression must be made upon crutches, by the aid of which all necessary exercise can be taken, and the tedium of confinement relieved. In the case of the carpus or lower extremity of the humerus, a similar plan of treatment must be pursued. At this stage a generous diet may be allowed; but stimulating drinks should, as a general rule, be strictly forbidden.

## STAGE OF EXUDATION.

The second stage of tuberculosis of bone is characterised by an exudation from the blood-vessels of the affected part. Not only does this exudation occur in the immediate vicinity of the vascular membrane of the cancelli, but it is likewise discovered in the lacunæ and canaliculi, to which the vessels of bone do not extend. In the latter case, the solid portion of the exudation is carried thither in a state of solution, and is subsequently deposited by a process similar to that of the nutrition of the ultimate tissue of bone. In a properly prepared section of bone which has undergone the second stage of tuberculous disease, we find that the morbid action is not confined to any particular part of the cancellous tissue; but that, on the contrary, the walls of the cancelli, the vascular membrane of the latter, their cavities, the lacunæ and their canaliculi, are alike the seat of deposit, although not equally so in point of frequency.

The process of tuberculous exudation in bone is, in every respect, similar to that which occurs in the pulmonary tissue,—namely, firstly, an exudation into the basement tissue of the vascular membrane of the cancelli, which may or may not extend into the lacunæ and canaliculi ; and secondly, the occupation, to a greater or less extent, of the cavities of the cancelli themselves. Hence, in a section of bone illustrative of this stage, we find that, in some cancelli, the vascular membrane, like that of the air-cells of the pulmonary tissue, has undergone a degree of thickening, and is more granular than in its healthy condition—that, in other cancelli, a portion of their cavities is occupied by deposit—whilst, in a third series, they are completely *stuffed* with this exudation. In the last mentioned condition the cancelli appear, under the microscope, as so many spaces of irregular size and shape, densely packed with exudation-matter in colour deeper than the bony fibres which constitute their walls.

FIGURE IV.

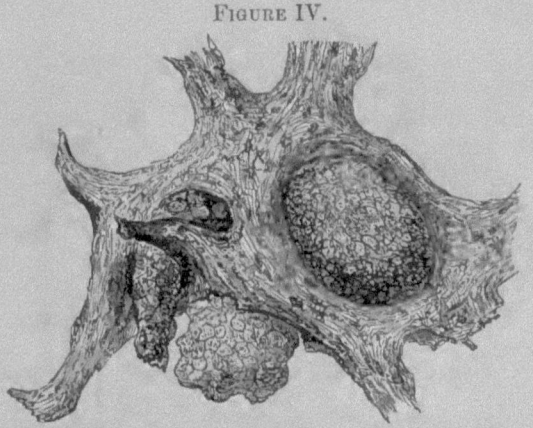

Fig. IV.—Tuberculous bone, showing the cancelli stuffed with exudation, which has undergone partial development into cells. Drawn under the Camera Lucida, by Mr Tuffen West.

On adding a drop of distilled water to the preparation, a quantity of granular matter of irregular shape, and varying in size from 1-7000th to 1-15,000th of an inch in diameter, and dark, irregular, granular patches, from 1-600th to 1-1300th of an inch in their long diameter, are detached from the cancelli, which are thereby rendered more transparent than before. In colour these patches vary from a light yellow to a dirty reddish-brown, which is no doubt due to the different degree of staining which they have undergone by the hæmatine of the blood extravasated into the respective cancelli. They consist of portions of the lining membrane of the latter detached during the process of exudation, and imprisoned amidst the tuberculous matter which occupies the cavities of the cancelli.

As they and the granular matter before mentioned lie *in situ* in their respective cancelli, a few oil-globules of various sizes are seen to be scattered amongst them ; whilst others lie on the surface of the osseous walls of these cavities. In this state the lacunæ of the latter are but dimly visible. On adding now a solution of potash to the preparation, the number of detached granules and patches increases, the cancelli becoming less and less occupied by the deposit, and the structure of the osseous walls of the latter more and more defined. There appears with this result a great increase in the number of oil-globules, which crowd different points of the field of vision, and the formation of which is contemporaneous with a marked diminution in the degree of opacity of the granular mat-ter and irregularly sized patches before named. It is thus evident, that the latter have, by a species of degeneration, undergone a degree of fatty transformation, which, in the further stage of the disease, is carried to a still greater extent.

FIGURE V.

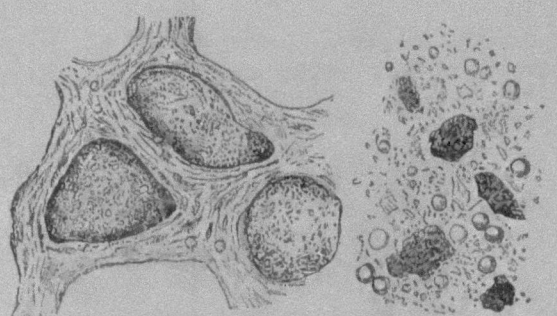

Fig. V.—Tuberculous bone after the action of liquor potassæ.

The action of æther is similar to that of liquor potassæ. The number of granular patches detached by the former, is, however, not so great, nor are the patches quite so transparent, as by the latter re-agent.

Acetic acid has the effect of rendering the cancelli, their contents, and the bony fibre more transparent.

In examining the naked walls of the cancelli after the removal of the contents of the latter, minute projections of bone, constituting exostoses, are not unfrequently observed to spring from them into the cavities of the cancelli (Fig. VI.). These vary in size from a minute elevation on the surface of the cancellous wall to an exos-tosis which occupies nearly the whole cavity of a cancellus. In this new bone lacunæ, similar to those of the real bony tissue itself, are sometimes to be seen. In the lacunæ and canaliculi of the real bony tissue, tuberculous and osseous deposits likewise occur. In the former deposit the lacunæ and canaliculi appear darker than in their healthy condition. By the action of a solution of potash or of æther, they are rendered lighter ; and here and there, after the addition of æther, may be seen a single drop of oil filling a lacuna. If to another specimen, in which the lacunæ and their canaliculi are occupied by tuberculous deposit, hydrochloric acid be added, the earthy matter producing the opacity of their walls is dissolved, their membranous outline is thereby rendered visible, whilst the tuberculous character of their contents is distinctly seen. By washing away the hydrochloric acid, and by subsequently adding a weak solution of potash, the contents of the lacunæ are broken up into granules and minute oil-globules; whilst the lacunæ themselves appear as irregularly transparent cells, scattered over with a number of minute and adherent granules.

Where the lacunæ and their canaliculi are occupied by bony deposit, they form objects of much darker appearance than the contiguous lacunæ and canaliculi which are not similarly affected. In this respect the contrast is very striking. That bony deposit does occupy the lacunæ and canaliculi, may be chemically determined by the action of a mineral acid, which causes, firstly, the canaliculi, then the dark circumference of the lacunæ, and lastly, their dark centre to dissolve, and to leave behind a faint, membranous outline of their previous existence. This positive demonstration is negatively proved by the action of a solution of potash, by æther, or by the spirit of turpentine, which produces no change whatever in the appearance of the lacunæ and canaliculi in question.

FIGURE VI.

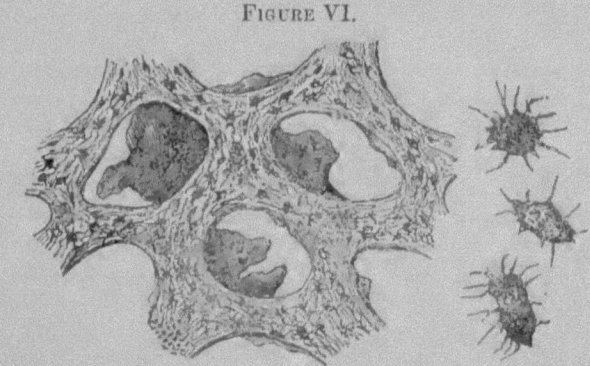

Fig. VI.—Tuberculous bone after the removal of the contents of the cancelli by boiling in æther. Osseous walls show the lacunæ and canaliculi more or less occupied by deposit. The cancelli exhibit exostoses springing from their margins. Separate lacunæ more highly magnified, and showing different degrees of occupation by deposit. Seen in spirit of turpentine.

It will thus be seen, that wherever the nutritive blastema can penetrate bone, there also tuberculous exudation occurs; and that, although due provision is made, by the system of lacunæ and canaliculi, for the proper nutrition of the ultimate tissue of bone, it is nevertheless evident, from the extra-vascular position of these, that their power of absorption must be extremely limited, and that any deposit within them can scarcely, if at all, admit of subsequent removal. Hence the explanation of the incurable character of tuberculosis of bone, when exudation has proceeded to the obliteration of its lacunæ and canaliculi. Fortunately, however, this obliteration is frequently confined to a portion only of the diseased tissue, which, for the reason of the extra-vascular position of the lacunæ and canaliculi before named, may either pass into abeyance, and thus remain for an indefinite time, or, should this result not take place, it may admit of removal by operative procedure with the prospect of recovery to the less diseased contiguous portions of bone.

The pathological changes, then, which attend the second stage of tuberculosis of bone, may, in *resumé*, be stated to be :—

  I. Exudation into the basement structure of the lining membrane of the cancelli, and consequent thickening of the latter.

 II. Exudation into the cancelli, with more or less consequent detachment of their lining membrane.

III. Obliteration, more or less, of the lacunæ and their canaliculi by tuberculous deposit.

 IV. The growth of exostoses from the osseous walls of the cancelli, and the occasional occupation of the lacunæ and canaliculi by osseous deposit.

The local symptoms which characterise this second stage of the disease are more or less acute, according to the tendency of the disease either to progress or to pass into abeyance. In the former instance, there are—enlargement of the affected part ; swelling of the superjacent soft parts, which are more or less elastic on pressure ; deformity ; increased heat and tenderness, aggravated by pressure or motion of the affected part ; often a slight blush of redness on the skin, which is usually pencilled with enlarged veins ; with deeply-seated nocturnal pains, or a sense of gnawing in the bone itself. These symptoms are attended by more or less loss of appetite, thirst, increased heat of skin, quickened pulse, wasting of flesh, loss of strength, wakefulness, and scanty and depraved secretions.

In the latter instance, the local symptoms are—enlargement of the bone itself, thickening of the superjacent soft parts, deformity, enlargement of the veins of the skin, little or no perceptible increase of temperature, some degree of pain on percussion, occasional sense of weight, aching, or of gnawing in the affected part, with more or less impediment to the free use of the neighbouring joint. The general symptoms are expressed in a certain loss of flesh ; pallor and, occasionally, haggard expression of countenance; variable appetite ; somewhat quick, small, and feeble pulse ; cool skin, and general absence of excitement in the system.

The following cases are related in illustration of the above statements :—

CASE IV.—H. W., aged 7 years, of nervo-bilious temperament, thin and spare, with predisposition to tuberculosis on the father's side, accidentally fell upon a knife, by which the right knee was cut and injured. The wound healed in good time, and for four months afterwards he continued to use the limb. During this time, however, the inner side of the knee-joint became gradually enlarged, pain on motion supervened, and at length the knee-joint flexed until the toes only rested upon the ground whilst standing or in the act of progression. On taking charge of the case, on the 13th of November 1850, I found, on examination, enlargement of the head of the right tibia, which was the seat of constant aching and uneasiness, and of frequent, sharp, lancinating pain. The enlargement was so confined to the head of the tibia, that the natural symmetry of the knee-joint was, in a great measure, destroyed by a protuberance on the inner side, which immediately arrested the attention. There was increased heat of the part, which was tender on pressure, and which betrayed a considerable degree of sensitiveness on passive motion of the knee-joint. The veins on the inner side of the joint were enlarged, the superjacent soft parts tense and elastic, the knee-joint itself was partly flexed, and the ham-string tendons were rigid and prominent. The body had gradually wasted since the occurrence of the accident ; the countenance was thin, pale, and emaciated ; the appetite deficient ; the tongue thinly coated with a dirty-white fur ; the alvine and urinary secretions were scanty and depraved ; the skin, cool during the greater part of the day, often became somewhat hot towards night ; the pulse was quickened, small, and feeble ; and the sleep was generally disturbed.

In the treatment, the patient, at the outset, was confined to bed ; the affected limb was laid at perfect rest ; six leeches were immediately applied to the most sensitive part ; and the bleeding from their bites was promoted, as long as possible, by flannels wrung out of hot poppy decoction, which was followed by the application of a hot bran poultice to the knee during the following night. Half a grain of mercury with chalk, two and a half grains of Dover's powder, and eight of sesquicarbonate of soda, were given every three hours ; whilst the diet was restricted to milk, weak tea or coffee, and the different farinacea. On the following day the knee was repeatedly fomented with the hot poppy decoction, and at night a blister was applied to the whole front and sides of the joint. The same medicines and diet were continued. This treatment was followed by considerable relief to the pain, which, together with other symptoms of local excitement, had subsided at the end of a fortnight. The knee-joint was now fixed by a posterior splint, the limb was rolled in starched bandages, and the patient put upon crutches. Two grains of iodide of potassium were given in a light vegetable infusion three times a-day ; the secretions of the liver and of the bowels were solicited by an occasional dose of grey powder, rhubarb, magnesia, and the sesquicarbonate of soda ; the circulation through the skin was promoted by daily tepid salt-water sponging ; and the diet consisted of animal food, milk, and other articles before named. By and bye, the iodide of potassium was discontinued, and three drachms of the cod-liver oil were administered every night and morning. At the end of seven weeks from the assumption of crutches, the motions of the knee-joint were performed without the slightest uneasiness, and nothing but the enlargement of the head of the tibia remained. All restrictions were now removed from the limb, the cod-liver oil was continued, and fresh air and a generous diet were enjoined. Two months afterwards the oil was discontinued, the patient was apparently in perfect health, and the mere enlargement of the head of the tibia alone remained.

CASE V.—H. M., aged 7 years, a girl of nervo-lymphatic temperament, with predisposition to tuberculosis on the mother's side, fell one day, and struck the right knee with some force upon the ground. From this time she experienced more or less uneasiness in the part, and a gradually increasing lameness set in. This attracted the attention of her parents, who, seven weeks after the accident, requested me to take charge of the case. At this time the right knee was generally enlarged to the extent of an increase of two inches in the circumference of the joint, which was partially flexed, and, to a certain extent, crippled in its movements. The enlargement existed more on the inner than on the outer side of the joint, the swelling was somewhat elastic on pressure, and manifested no uneasiness except over the head of the tibia. Here the integuments were somewhat hotter than natural, and betrayed a degree of tenderness on pressure, which was aggravated by deeper pressure upon the head of the bone. Examination of this part left no doubt of its enlargement ; whilst the statements of the patient herself showed that it was the seat of many uneasy sensations, particularly on motion of the limb, and during the night. The effect of this condition on the general system, was read in the pale, haggard expression of countenance ; loss of flesh ; soft, flabby condition of the muscles ; small, feeble, quick pulse ; diminished appetite ; and in the imperfect discharge of the digestive and other functions.

With the view of relieving the heat and tenderness over the head of the tibia, the application of four leeches was advised ; but the determined obstinacy of the patient overcame the wavering resolution of the parents, and no abstraction of blood in consequence took place. Perfect rest, however, in the horizontal posture, repeated fomentations of hot poppy decoction, bran poultices enveloping the whole joint, the use of mercury with chalk, Dover's powder, and the sesquicarbonate of soda, and a milk and farinaceous diet, subdued the more active symptoms in the course of a fortnight. The limb was now confined by a posterior splint and starched bandages, and the patient put upon crutches. A good diet without stimulants was allowed, and three teaspoonfuls of cod-liver oil were administered immediately after the morning and evening meals. In eight weeks the splint and bandages were cast aside, the soft structures of the knee-joint had returned to their natural condition, and the head of the tibia was free from uneasiness either on percussion or in the attempt at progression. A degree of fulness, however, was visible over this part, which was evidently due to enlargement of the head of the tibia, and which gave to the limb at this point a circumferential increase of nearly half an inch over the corresponding point of the opposite limb. Six months have now elapsed since all treatment was discontinued ; there has hitherto been no return of the disease ; and the patient, notwithstanding the continuance of the tibial enlargement before named, remains in the perfect use of the limb.

CASE VI.—B. S., aged 23 years, of bilio-lymphatic temperament, married, mother of three children, whilst stepping from a railway carriage in the autumn of 1854, suddenly felt, at the moment the right foot touched the ground, a sensation as though something had given way in the corresponding instep. She experienced for a few minutes great pain in the part, which, by and bye, subsided in a great measure, and she walked a distance of nearly two miles to her home. For several weeks afterwards she continued to use the foot, which, however, was scarcely ever free from some degree of uneasiness, particularly during the night. A few days after alighting from the railway carriage, she observed, for the first time, swelling of the instep. The foot continuing to get worse, a neighbouring surgeon undertook the treatment of the case, which, with certain remissions and aggravations of symptoms, continued under his care until the winter of 1857-8. On January 10th, 1858, the further treatment of the case was confided to me. At this time the whole dorsum of the foot was swollen, to the extent of an increase of five inches over the circumference of the left ; the skin was tense, elastic on pressure, pencilled with veins meandering in various directions over the surface, was somewhat hotter than natural, and presented, at several points, a faintly bluish appearance ; whilst, at others, and especially over the scaphoid bone, it manifested the faintest erythematous blush. Pressure at various points, passive motion, or any attempt to use the foot in progression, aggravated the pain, which was more or less constantly present. This was more severe during the night than in the day, and bore the different characters of a gnawing, boring, aching, breaking, and twisting pain. The general system expressed a pale, haggard, dull, faintly sallow countenance ; a large, flabby, dirty-white tongue ; defective appetite ; no thirst ; sluggishness of the bowels ; scanty, highly-coloured urine, but depositing no sediment ; and a moderately cool skin. The pulse ranged from 80 to 90 per minute, was small, sharp, and somewhat excitable ; the sleep was broken and disturbed ; and the disposition of the mind was to the gloomy and foreboding. She knew but little of the history of her immediate relatives ; nevertheless she stated, that two of her sisters had died of pulmonary consumption.

In the treatment of the case the foot was laid at perfect rest on a level with the body ; any attempt to walk upon it was strictly forbidden ; to relieve the local excitement and pain, six leeches were applied, and these were followed by the application of a blister to the whole dorsum of the foot. Two grains of the iodide of potassium in an ounce of the decoction of sarsaparilla, and a pill, containing one grain each of the mercury with chalk and the compound extract of colocynth, with four-sixths of a grain of opium, were given three times a-day. The diet for some days consisted of milk and the different farinacea, to which animal food was subsequently added. The treatment was continued without any modification until the following March, when, owing to a tenderness of the gums, which had existed for a fortnight, the mercury with chalk was omitted from the pills. During this time the foot had undergone a steady improvement in the abatement of the local pain and the gradual subsidence of the swelling ; the countenance had, in a great measure, lost its expression of haggard anxiety ; the tongue had become clean ; the appetite regular and good ; the bowels natural in their action ; and the sleep sound and refreshing. The foot was now supported by a sling from the neck, the patient put upon crutches, active exercise was enjoined, and the same diet and medicines were continued. By June the foot, with the exception of a certain degree of enlargement of its dorsum, had returned to its natural condition, the patient could both stand and walk upon it without the least uneasiness, and the general health was re-established.

The indications of treatment, which flow from the foregoing pathological considerations of the exudative stage of tuberculosis of bone, have for their object—

I. To remove active congestion when it exists.

II. To promote the absorption of exudation from the affected tissue.

In every instance, in which the disease is progressing, active congestion, to a greater or less extent, co-exists with tuberculous exudation in bone ; therefore, in the treatment of the second stage of tuberculosis of this structure, the remedies applicable to the first stage are, to a certain extent, demanded. These are local depletion, frequently repeated anodyne fomentations, absolute rest of the affected part, and counter-irritation.

It will be seen, in the relation of the above cases, that, in the second stage of tuberculosis of bone, the structures of the neighbouring joints are generally more or less involved ; and that the remedies applicable to the fulfilment of the former of the above indications, are also eminently calculated to subdue the co-existing excitement in these articular tissues. They ought, therefore, to be perseveringly and rigidly carried out, in the manner before stated, until the symptoms of active congestion, as well of the bony tissue as of the neighbouring structures, have entirely disappeared. This having been done, and further exudation having thereby been prevented, the efforts of treatment are next to be directed to the fulfilment of the second indication, in promoting, as far as possible, the absorption of the exudation which has already taken place. This object is best effected by the exhibition of those medicines which are known from experience to exert an alterative effect upon the system—to favour the liquefaction of exudations—to allay pain and nervous excitement—and to promote the healthy discharge of the bodily functions. Amongst such remedies, mercury in the form of grey powder, the alkalies, particularly potash in combination with iodine, opium and its different preparations, cod-liver oil, iron, and the different vegetable tonics, deserve to be specified. The use of mercury with chalk in small doses, extending over a lengthened period, and given in conjunction with opium, iodide of potassium, and a light vegetable bitter, is often attended by the happiest result. While it were unquestionably better, for the constitutional powers of the patient, not to carry the use of this preparation of mercury to the extent of complete ptyalism, it is nevertheless to be observed, that the induction of a slight tenderness of the gums by this remedy, and the maintenance of this condition for a short time, will, in many instances, be followed by a much more rapid and beneficial effect upon the local disease than where no such tenderness of the gums has been produced. Such extended use of the grey powder is, however, only admissible in those cases which threaten to run a determined course, and in which the natural vigour and energy of the system have not been entirely broken down. In other instances its use must be limited to its alterative effect; whilst the more prominent place is given to cod-liver oil, iron, and the other remedies previously named. In all instances, in which the tongue is clean, the skin cool, the pulse small and feeble, and the body emaciated, cod-liver oil, and the different preparations of iron with vegetable tonics, are indicated. Their use, however, must be closely watched, inasmuch as it occasionally happens that, notwithstanding their perfect agreement with the system for a time, fresh local excitement supervenes on their continued exhibition, which ought, therefore, to be regarded as a certain indication of the necessity for their immediate withdrawal.

To favour the action of the above agents upon the general system, to restore the general health and vigour of the body, and thereby to affect beneficially the local disease, *exercise* is of paramount importance in the treatment of this stage. This, to a certain extent, should be of an active character; but when the lower extremity is the one affected, active exercise, provided the diseased part were not placed beyond the control of the patient, would quickly excite a fresh accession of mischief, which would not only defeat the object in view, but which might compromise the safety of the limb. It is, therefore, absolutely necessary, in every such case in which active exercise is proper, to place the diseased part beyond the *will* of the patient, and the possibility of its being used. A surgeon who should neglect this precaution, would, in my opinion, be guilty of a dereliction of one of the most important duties which attach to the treatment of this stage. Wherever the use of the diseased part can be prevented by the application of splints and starched bandages, these ought invariably to be employed; because they not only render motion of the part impracticable, but they steady and support the neighbouring joints, whilst the equal pressure of the bandages tends to prevent the recurrence of active congestion, and to promote the absorption of exudation-matter in the soft superjacent tissues of the diseased bone. They ought also to be employed for some time after the *apparent* recovery of the patient, and for this reason—the vessels of bone are extremely slow in returning to their natural caliber and contractility; they are, therefore, in doing so, posterior in time to those of the superjacent soft parts, from the condition of which, inference, as to the state of the osseous tissue, is derived—their proneness to relapse is correspondingly great—and they consequently require, after the removal of the more visible signs of disease from the soft parts, a continuance, for a time, of the above means of restraint. In some cases splints and bandages, or even the latter only, cannot be borne. When this happens, as is more frequently the case in the tarsus, the corresponding limb ought, during exercise, to be suspended by a sling, which not only prevents the uneasy sensation which would be produced by the force of gravity, but which constantly reminds the patient of the necessity for maintaining a continued desuetude of the affected part.

To the use of issues, moxas, setons, and open blisters in the immediate neighbourhood of the disease, strong objection exists on the ground that they would prevent the application of splints and bandages, from which a much more beneficial effect may, in the manner before stated, be obtained.

When circumstances are favourable, removal of the patient to the sea-coast sometimes greatly contributes to recovery, which, in other instances, would be promoted by a lengthened residence at Leamington, and by the judicious use of those of its waters which have, by recent analysis, been shown to be somewhat rich in iodine.

Throughout the whole treatment of this second stage, particular attention should be given to *food* and *drink*. These, at the commencement, will generally require to be of an unstimulating kind, as milk, the different farinacea, and the various white meats, to which the red meats, and sometimes the moderate use of malt liquor or wine, may, when all local excitement has entirely ceased, be added. Attention, too, is further required to *sleep* and the condition of the *skin*. The former allays excitability, refreshes the nervous system, and invigorates every organ; whilst the daily ablution of the latter maintains, in a healthy condition, its important function, increases the activity of its circulation, and thereby not only contributes to the relief of local congestions, but also to the increased aëration of the blood and the vivifying properties of that fluid.

## STAGE OF GERMINATION AND ULCERATION.

The third stage of tuberculosis of bone is marked by the germination and development of the exudation which occurred in the previous stage, and by the effect of that development upon the osseous and contiguous tissues.  Owing to the limited space which the cancelli offer to the exudation, to the dense accumulation of the latter within their cavities, and to the consequent pressure upon the blood-vessels distributed upon their walls, the circulation through the capillaries of the cancelli is, in a great measure, arrested, or entirely stopped. From this condition two pathological results occur,—namely, the arrest, more or less complete, of the nutrition of the ultimate tissue of bone, and the imperfect development of the exudation within the cancelli.   The more distant the seat of exudation from the source of vascular supply to the cancelli, the more palpably are the above two conditions effected.   Hence, by way of illustration, the exudation within the centre of a short bone, or, in the head of a long bone, at a point equidistant from the termination of the medullary canal and the periosteum, does not acquire that development into cells as exudation immediately contiguous to the latter.   The sole cause of this is, the diminished or arrested circulation through these distant portions of bone, and the consequent absence of the necessary conditions for germination and growth.   In proportion, therefore, to this partial or complete arrest of the circulation are the diminished vitality of the corresponding portions of the cancellous tissue, and the inability of the exudation to acquire a cell-formation.   These conditions are highly favourable to the disintegration of the one and the fatty transformation of the other; but so long as oxygen is excluded, neither disintegration nor metamorphosis can take place. When, however, this oxygen has, either by a certain amount of continuance of the circulation, or by a *direct* communication between the tuberculous bone and the air, gained admission to the diseased parts, rapid disintegration of the bony texture and rapid transformation of the exudation may occur.   Under this process, the walls of the cancelli disintegrate from the surface towards the centre of each partition, which in consequence becomes thinner and thinner, until at length it is entirely destroyed.   Two cancelli are now broken into one; and this process continuing in other contiguous partitions, an excavation, involving the destruction of many cancelli, is at length produced.   During this progressive destruction of the walls of the cancelli, a striking difference occurs between the diameters of the cancelli themselves and their osseous partitions which are thus affected, and those of healthy cancellous bone.   This difference is much more palpably appreciated by a comparison of the healthy and diseased cancellous tissue under the microscope or in sketch, than by any comparisons of the difference of their respective diameters without such ocular demonstration.

FIGURE VII.

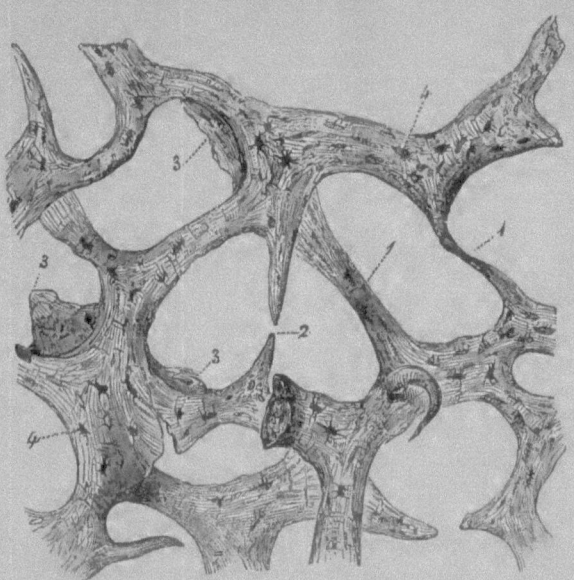

Fig. VII.—1. Cancellous walls greatly reduced in diameter by progressive disintegration.

2. A cancellous wall completely disintegrated at one point, showing the process of conversion of two cancelli into one.

3. Exostoses springing from the walls of the cancelli.

4. Lacunæ stuffed with tuberculous and osseous deposit.

Drawn under the Camera Lucida, by Mr Tuffen West.

From the above Figure, in comparison with Figure II., it will be seen that, during the above stage of tuberculosis of bone, the diameters of the cancelli increase in proportionate ratio to the diminution of those of their osseous walls by the disintegration of the latter, and that they both bear to those of healthy cancellous bone the following relations, as determined by mean measurement :—

MEAN DIAMETERS OF CANCELLI OF TUBERCULOUS BONE IN THE ULCERATIVE STAGE.

|  | Long Diameter. | Short Diameter. |
|---|---|---|
| A | $14\frac{1}{2}$ | 12 |
| B | 24 | 14 |
| C | 24 | 18 |
| D | 37 | 23 |
| E | $16\frac{1}{2}$ | $10\frac{1}{2}$ |
| F | 22 | $10\frac{1}{2}$ |
| G | 19 | 16 |
| H | 24 | $22\frac{1}{2}$ |
| I | $29\frac{1}{2}$ | 22 |
| K | 27 | $11\frac{1}{2}$ |
|  | $237\frac{1}{2}$ | 160 |
| Mean average, | $23\frac{7.5}{1000}$ths inch. | $\frac{16}{1000}$ths inch. |

MEAN DIAMETERS OF THE OSSEOUS WALLS OF TUBERCULOUS BONE IN THE
ULCERATIVE STAGE.

| | | | |
|---|---|---|---|
| *a* | . | . | $7\frac{1}{2}$ |
| *b* | . | . | $4\frac{1}{2}$ |
| *c* | . | . | $2\frac{1}{2}$ |
| *d* | . | . | $3\frac{1}{2}$ |
| *e* | . | . | $2$ |
| *f* | . | . | $4\frac{1}{2}$ |
| *g* | . | . | $3$ |
| *h* | . | . | $4\frac{1}{2}$ |
| *i* | . | . | $4\frac{3}{4}$ |
| *j* | . | . | $4\frac{1}{2}$ |
| *k* | . | . | $3$ |
| *l* | . | . | $3$ |
| *m* | . | . | $3$ |
| *n* | . | . | $5$ |
| *o* | . | . | $5$ |
| *p* | . | . | $2\frac{1}{2}$ |
| *q* | . | . | $5$ |
| *r* | . | . | $4\frac{1}{2}$ |
| *s* | . | . | $4\frac{1}{2}$ |
| *t* | . | . | $1\frac{1}{4}$ |

$$\overline{\phantom{xxx}}$$
$$78$$

Mean average,        $\frac{3\cdot16}{1000}$ths inch.

Whilst the destruction of the walls of the cancelli is progressing,
as above shown, the exudation within the cancelli themselves,
unable, from the absence of the circulation, to derive the pabulum
of nutrition for its perfect development into cells, undergoes fatty
degeneration. Hence, the microscopic examination of bone, which
has undergone these pathological changes, shows partial or complete destruction of the walls of the cancelli (Figure VII.); whilst
the contents of such cancelli consist of oil-globules of various sizes
from a metamorphosis of a portion of the exudation, masses of exudation-matter more or less converted into fat, granular matter and
patches of the lining membrane of the cancelli in a similar condition, together with the ultimate earthy particles of disintegrated
bone (Figure V.).

As the deposit of tuberculous matter is not of equal amount
throughout the affected cancelli, so neither does the process of
ulceration in them observe the same period of time or the same
ratio. The greater the amount of exudation within the cancelli,
and the nearer this is to the source of vascular supply, the sooner
does ulceration take place. Hence, the surface of a short bone,
and next to this, in a long bone, the immediate neighbourhood of
the termination of the medullary canal, are the seats at which
ulceration, in tuberculosis of bone, first occurs. In the former,
exudation into the superjacent soft parts, and its subsequent
germination, growth, and degeneration, constitute abscesses, which
open a communication between the surface and the diseased bone.
In the latter, this condition of the superjacent soft parts may not
occur until the exudation in the cancelli, near the termination of

the medullary canal, has already germinated, attained its cell-growth, and degenerated into pus-corpuscles. In this manner, an abscess, confined within the substance of the bone, may exist for some time without any communication with the external air. This communication, however, at length takes place; and the external air, admitted, in consequence, into free contact with the tuberculous bone, its oxygen hastens the degeneration of the exudation, and the disintegration of the diseased bone. When oxygen gains access to the exudation within the cancelli, without the continuance of the circulation through the capillaries of the latter, such exudation undergoes fatty transformation with but little previous manifestation of cell-development; but where a continuance of the circulation through the cancelli is maintained in conjunction with the free admission of air to their contained exudation, the latter is first developed into cells, and then, as cells, transformed into pus. Pus, therefore, is *never seen* as a constituent of the contents of cancelli, which are *stuffed* with tuberculous exudation, which lie *within* the substance of a bone, and the circulation of which has been *obliterated*. But around these cancelli, in others which are but partially occupied by deposit, and in which the capillary circulation still exists, the conditions for the germination and growth of the exudation continue; the latter is in consequence developed into cells, which subsequently, by the action of oxygen, degenerate and become pus-corpuscles. It will thus be seen that, for the commencement of the process of softening, as arising out of cell-development, a certain amount or continuance of the circulation is necessary, and that where this is entirely arrested, this kind of softening cannot take place. In some parts of a tuberculous bone the cancelli are choked, as it were, with exudation, and the circulation is entirely obliterated; whilst the surrounding cancelli are but partly occupied by deposit, and in them the circulation is, to a certain extent, maintained. Where there is no circulation there is no *softening*, in the above acceptation of that term; and as there is no circulation through a tuberculous mass formed by a number of contiguous cancelli stuffed with exudation, it is certain that the above-mentioned form of softening does not, and cannot, commence in the midst or interior of such a mass. It must, therefore, commence at the *circumference;* and, in this respect, it observes in bone the same process and situation as tuberculosis in the pulmonary tissue. Like the latter disease, too, an excavation, once formed in the cancellous tissue of bone, increases by the continued exudation in its walls, by the subsequent germination, growth, and degeneration of such exudation, and by the consequent disintegration of the ultimate tissue of bone.

When the deposit of tubercle is unequal throughout the cancelli of the same bone, when, in consequence, there are, as it were, islets of bone, the cancelli of which are choked with exudation, whilst the cancelli of the intervening portions of bone are but partially occupied by deposit, the process of softening may commence at the circumference of each of such islets, and, in this way, separate and distinct excavations, as in the pulmonary tissue, may occur. When, again, the tuberculous exudation is limited to a certain number of the cancelli, the latter, by the germination and growth of the exudation, may be destroyed; but the circulation of the surrounding cancelli remaining, a plastic exudation may take place upon the surface of such excavation, and thus a healing process is established. It will readily be seen, that it is in the last-recited extent of the disease that the removal, by operative procedure, of the tuberculous portion of bone is likely to be followed by a happy result; whilst, on the other hand, it is manifestly apparent, that where the tuberculous exudation has invaded the whole or the greater number of the cancelli of a bone, resection or amputation is the only means which promises a favourable result.

It has already been stated, that, during the progress of tuberculosis of bone, the adjacent articular structures become similarly affected; and, as the process of ulceration occurs in the latter, it is, as a general rule, by extension of the disease from the extremity of the bone to the adherent cartilage, and thence to the other structures of the joint. As a preparatory step, however, to the ulceration of the cartilage, an exudation is thrown out between it and the extremity of the bone by the vessels of the latter, and this exudation, undergoing a certain development into cells, constitutes a seemingly false membrane, to which important functions, in the subsequent destruction of the cartilage, have been ascribed. Of itself, and by virtue of an inherent property, this false membrane has no power to cause the absorption of the cartilage; but, by interposing between it and the bone, from the vessels of which the cartilage draws its pabulum of support, the healthy nutrition of the latter is destroyed, and its subsequent ulceration is in consequence decreed. It is extremely rare to find this false membrane intervening between the whole extent of the cartilage and the adjacent bone. It much more commonly exists in patches, and these invariably correspond with diseased points of bone beneath. Where the cartilage is yet adherent to the bone, no such false membrane is to be found, and the condition of the bone beneath is proportionately normal.

Hence, the formation of this false membrane is but the natural result of the advance of the disease to the surface of the articulating extremity of the bone; and the subsequent destruction of the cartilage is no more ascribable to the influence of any power of absorption on its part, than is the destruction of the periosteum, or of the superjacent soft tissues, to an inherent power of absorption in the exudation which occurs beneath the former, and amongst the latter, in the progress of the disease to the surface of the body. The true explanation, then, seems to be, that where, in the progress of the ulcerative stage of tuberculosis of bone, the cartilages of the adjacent joints ulcerate, they, in a great measure, do so as the result of an exudation thrown out between them and their corresponding extremities of bone by the vessels of the latter, by which their normal nutrition is destroyed, and their subsequent disintegration induced. I say, " in a great measure;" because the ulceration of the cartilages is not entirely due to the effect of intervening exudation, but in part to tuberculous disease of the cartilages themselves. If, in such cases, a perpendicular section of a cartilage, at its unattached point, be examined in the microscope, it will be found, that the cells of its lowest portion are apparently increased in number—that they lie with their long diameter parallel to the surface of the cartilage—that they are larger than the cells of healthy cartilage—and that they are more or less crowded with granules, which manifest the chemical characteristics of oil according to the degree of metamorphosis which they have undergone. Some of these cells have burst, and discharged their granular contents into the surrounding hyaline substance; whilst, at other points, between cells which have not yet discharged their contents, granules are deposited, in variable number, in the substance of the cartilage. In the middle portion of such cartilage, the disposition of the cells is somewhat different. Instead of finding them arranged with their long diameter parallel to the surface of the cartilage, they generally observe, in this respect, an angle from 45° to 85°, whilst they are less crowded with granules than those of the portion of cartilage subjacent to them. Notwithstanding this, they are widely different, in this respect, to the cells of healthy cartilage; whilst the intervening hyaline substance, although dimly granular in many points, is less so than that of the lowest stratum of this structure. If the examination of the cartilage be carried to its synovial surface, it will be found that the same pathological condition of its cells, the same parallel arrangement of their long diameter to its surface, and the same process of disintegration, as were observed in the opposite surface, may exist. This surface, however, may or may not as yet have undergone ulceration; for, where the tuberculosis commences in the adjacent bone, and thence extends to the contiguous joint, ulceration of the synovial surface of the cartilage is, as a general rule, posterior in time to ulceration of the opposite surface. When, on the other hand, tuberculosis commences in the synovial membrane, the contiguous surface of the cartilage is the one to be thus primarily affected. When such is the case, ulceration is preceded by an exudation between the synovial membrane and the subjacent surface of the cartilage, which is poured out by the vessels of the former, and which, by its subsequent development into cells, constitutes, as in the case of ulceration of the opposite surface of the cartilage, a false membrane, to the influence of which the ulceration of the contiguous surface of the cartilage has been ascribed. Here again, as in the opposite surface of the cartilage, this false membrane has no innate power of determining ulceration in the cartilage beneath; but, by interposing between the latter and the vessels which ramify on the surface of the synovial membrane, from which the contiguous surface of the cartilage draws its nutritive blastema, it obstructs the healthy nutrition of the latter, and thus favours its subsequent disintegration. If, at the time this exudation takes place, the air were freely admitted to it, instead of passing into a false membrane of nucleated cells, the latter would be converted into pus-corpuscles, and as such they would be discharged through the different sinuses communicating with their seat. Such, indeed, is their destination when this free access of oxygen to them has been accomplished. It is, therefore, the *conditions* under which they exist, rather than their vital tendency, which determine them to the formation of a false membrane; and the laws of vital dynamics teach, that structures, formed and existing under such conditions, can exert no special and individual action upon the tissues of the surrounding organism. If such were not the case, we should, in the foregoing instance, expect that a false membrane would be formed between the whole extent of the synovial membrane and the subjacent cartilage on which it is intended to operate; because, where nature designs a structure for a special purpose, it gives it an uninterrupted anatomical development commensurate with its physiological requirements. In contravention of this law, we find, in the case of the false membrane before cited, that, instead of existing throughout the whole extent of the surface of the cartilage, it exists only at those points of it where ulceration is either present or about to commence, and that it is absent from all other portions of its surface. This pathological fact seems, therefore, to show, that its presence is without design, and that its existence is the *result*, and not the *cause*, of those conditions which determine the ulceration of the cartilage.

Although, in this advanced stage of tuberculosis of bone, the extension of ulceration to the adjacent cartilage is generally first manifested by the attached surface of the latter, yet it not unfrequently happens, that the synovial surface is the one primarily affected. This may occur when, shortly after the commencement of the disease in the bone, tuberculosis of the synovial membrane of the neighbouring joint supervenes, which may lead to ulceration of the subjacent surface of the cartilage before the disease in the bone has had time to extend to the attached surface of that structure.

In the chemical composition of bone, as well as in its structural relations, important changes occur during the progress of the ulcerative stage. Thus a comparison of the following analyses of tuberculous bone with those of the healthy structure, as detailed in a previous page, shows that tuberculosis gives rise—

I. To a considerable increase of fat in the diseased bone.

II. To a large diminution of the salts of lime.

III. To a diminution in the organic matrix.

IV. To an increase in the soluble salts.

Composition of the condyles of the femur in the ulcerative stage of tuberculosis :—

| Organic Matter. | 1st Specimen. Female, age 24 years. | 2d Specimen. Female, age 10 years. | 3d Specimen. Male, age 29 years. |
|---|---|---|---|
| Cartilage and vessels, | 11·51 | 9·78 | 11·90 |
| Fat, | 69·24 | 74·85 | 67·36 |
| Inorganic Matter. | | | |
| Phosphate of lime with fluoride (?) of calcium, | 16·44 | 12·76 | 18·00 |
| Carbonate of lime, | 1·90 | 1·62 | 1·90 |
| Phosphate of magnesia, | ·20 | ·23 | ·21 |
| Soluble salts, | ·71 | ·76 | ·63 |
| | 100·00 | 100·00 | 100·00 |

Composition of the head of the tibia in the ulcerative stage of tuberculosis.

| Organic Matter. | 1st Specimen. Male, age 21 years. | 2d Specimen. Male, age 8 years. | 3d Specimen. Female, age 10 years. |
|---|---|---|---|
| Cartilage and vessels, | 9·63 | 9·08 | 9·17 |
| Fat, | 72·65 | 74·76 | 73·95 |
| Inorganic Matter. | | | |
| Phosphate of lime with fluoride (?) of calcium, | 14·73 | 13·21 | 13·73 |
| Carbonate of lime, | 1·87 | 1·75 | 1·90 |
| Phosphate of magnesia, | ·19 | ·15 | ·15 |
| Soluble salts, | ·93 | 1·05 | 1·10 |
| | 100·00 | 100·00 | 100·00 |

Composition of the astragalus in the ulcerative stage of tuberculosis :—

| Organic Matter. | 1st Specimen. Female, age 15 years. | 2d Specimen. Male, age 12 years. | 3d Specimen. Male, age 8 years. |
|---|---|---|---|
| Cartilage and vessels, | 17·02 | 9·97 | 14·95 |
| Fat, | 56·76 | 76·98 | 63·33 |
| Inorganic Matter. | | | |
| Phosphate of lime with fluoride (?) of calcium, | 22·04 | 10·51 | 18·10 |
| Carbonate of lime, | 3·05 | 1·37 | 2·69 |
| Phosphate of magnesia, | ·37 | ·17 | ·31 |
| Soluble salts, | ·76 | 1·00 | ·62 |
| | 100·00 | 100·00 | 100·00 |

Composition of the os calcis in the ulcerative stage of tuberculosis :—

| Organic Matter. | 1st Specimen. Female, age 10 years. | 2d Specimen. Male, age 12 years. | 3d Specimen. Male, age 8 years. |
|---|---|---|---|
| Cartilage and vessels, | 7·91 | 8·75 | 13·41 |
| Fat, | 81·63 | 79·59 | 70·18 |
| Inorganic Matter. | | | |
| Phosphate of lime with fluoride (?) of calcium, | 8·16 | 9·27 | 13·22 |
| Carbonate of lime, | ·97 | 1·07 | 1·87 |
| Phosphate of magnesia, | ·10 | ·12 | ·25 |
| Soluble salts, | 1·23 | 1·20 | 1·07 |
| | 100·00 | 100·00 | 100·00 |

Now, the increase of fat above shown, in the third stage of tuberculosis of bone, is no doubt due to the metamorphosis of the exudation contained within the cancelli; whilst the diminution of the salts of lime is referrible to a vital change in the organic matrix of the bone, by which the cohesion between that matrix and the ultimate earthy particles is destroyed, and the latter in consequence are liberated and set free. Hence, the diminished specific gravity and the great softness of tuberculous bone which has undergone the ulcerative stage. In all cases, in this stage, the disintegration of the cancellous walls reduces the quantitive proportion of cartilage below the standard of healthy bone; nevertheless the relative proportion of organic matrix to the earthy salts of tuberculous bone *equals*, and, generally, greatly *exceeds*, the relation which these two constituents bear to each other in health. An explanation of this result is probably read in the structural character of the fibro-gelatinous matrix, in its slow subjection to the influence of oxygen, and in the particular character of the earthy particles and their mode of combination with the organic basis of bone. A mineral acid removes entirely the calcareous salts of bone from the cartilaginous matrix, and leaves the morphological character of the latter intact. Incineration, on the other hand, destroys the organic basis, and leaves the ultimate earthy particles unaffected. Hence, the two are not in chemical combination to constitute bone; but, on the contrary, the organic material forms a nidus, through which the earthy particles are distributed, and thus, by a *vital* influence, which pervades every living structure, they are held together, and evince the peculiar characters of bone. Whilst, however, the organic basis manifests no elementary structural formations beyond fibres, the earthy particles have a definite shape and size. Hence, in the separation of the two by the death of bone, the organic matter is wasted by inappreciably microscopical proportions; whilst the earthy particles are set free without change or diminution in size. This mode of disintegration gives a relatively greater loss of the calcareous salts than of the organic matter, and thus accounts for the great diminution in the salts of lime, which the previous analyses show to exist in the ulcerative stage of tuberculosis of bone.

The local symptoms which attend the above stage are those of the previous stage, with the addition of those which depend on the formation of pus within the bone, in the tissues superjacent to it, or in both. Where the disease has run an active course, there are now active congestion around the tuberculous deposit and in the tissues superjacent to the bone, increased swelling, pain, tenderness, and inability to move the affected limb without considerable suffering. Pus approaches the surface at one or more points, preceded by pain of a throbbing, shooting, lancinating, or gnawing character —by diminished mobility of the part—by restless nights—and by more or less disturbance in the general system. At length the skin is elevated in circumscribed portions, becomes red, tense, and affords, on manipulation, the sensation of fluctuation beneath. It now gives way, and a discharge of pus mixed with blood takes place. For a brief period the more urgent symptoms are less exquisite; but the air finding access to the interior of the diseased bone, a rapid degeneration of the tuberculous exudation occurs, fresh excitement in the superjacent parts takes place, pus in increased quantity is produced, and the disease hastens, as it were, to the destruction of both life and limb. In this rapid course the local heat and tenderness are very great; the skin around the openings of the sinuses is red; the edges of the latter are ragged, irregular, and undermined; and the pus is thin, bloody, ichorous, and often gritty to the feel from the presence of the earthy particles of bone. The general symptoms, at this moment, are expressed by a hot and dry skin; quick, small, and feeble pulse; considerable thirst; loss of appetite; a clean, florid, shining tongue, smooth from the loss of its epithelium, and frequently with its papillæ apparently enlarged; diarrhœa; and scanty, highly-coloured urine, depositing a copious sediment of urates; together with hectic fever towards the latter part of the day.

In other cases not so acute, the urgency of both local and general symptoms is less marked; the edges of the sinuses are neither ragged nor undermined; but, on the contrary, they become thickened and everted, with depression of the surrounding skin; the pus, unequal in consistence and more or less curdy, is less bloody; and the general system is competent to the moderate discharge of its various functions.

In a third class of cases the symptoms are almost entirely local. There is little or no pain in the affected part, except on use or manipulation; the sensations arising out of the disease are more those of enlargement and incumbrance; the tissues above the diseased bone are thickened; the skin is cool, and depressed around the sinuses, which exhibit hard, everted edges; and the pus, scanty in quantity, is of variable consistence and colour. The tongue is moist, and either clean or covered with a thin, white fur; there is no thirst; the appetite is often regular; but the bowels are frequently torpid. The countenance is usually pale; the general surface cool; the pulse regular, soft, equal, and not accelerated; and the sleep undisturbed.

The following cases illustrate the above positions:—

CASE VII.—T. E., a girl aged 10 years, of nervo-sanguineous temperament, with light hair and eyes, and regular but stunted features, was admitted into the Chesterfield Hospital, on Sept. 5, 1856, for tuberculous disease of the knee-joint. Twelve months before admission, she received a blow on the knee from a stone thrown at her by a boy. She was ever afterwards lame of the joint, which gradually enlarged, and ultimately inflamed, suppurated, and rendered her unable to walk.

The knee, on admission to hospital, was flexed almost at a right angle, and was greatly enlarged from thickening of the soft tissues; the bony prominences were lost; and there were sinuses above, below, and on the outer side of the joint, from which a thin, curdy, unhealthy pus, sometimes mixed with blood, escaped. There was constant pain, which was greatly increased on any motion of the joint. She had lost flesh, had now a variable appetite, little or no thirst, no hectic, and the bowels were regular.

For five weeks she was enjoined perfect rest in bed, during which time the knee was treated with warm-water dressing and bread-sop poultices. The diet consisted of milk, light puddings, and, whenever the state of the system permitted, of a moderate quantity of animal food. For a short time there was an improvement in the local symptoms; but ultimately the case grew worse: the knee became exquisitely tender; the skin hot, red, and inflamed in patches; the edges of the sinuses thin, ragged, and surrounded by a bright, florid blush; whilst a thin, bloody, ichorous discharge constantly escaped through their openings. There were now headache, sickness, thirst, diarrhœa, hot skin, burning of the palms and of the soles of the feet; quick, small, and rapid pulse, and other symptoms of well-marked hectic.

At a consultation with my colleagues, it was decided to remove the limb. On the 17th of November, I performed amputation of the thigh whilst the patient was under the influence of chloroform. Three vessels required ligature. The flaps, except at the point of exit of the ligatures, united by the first intention. On the seventh day, two of the ligatures came away; on the tenth, the femoral ligature separated; and on the thirteenth, the stump had quite healed. The patient was shortly afterwards discharged from hospital in perfect health.

*Appearance of the diseased joint.*—The synovial membrane is of a pale yellow colour, thickened, pulpy, and apparently in a state of fatty degeneration. Where reflected over the cartilages of the joint, it can be scraped off as a semi-transparent jelly. The crucial ligaments are partly destroyed. The cartilage on the outer condyle of the femur is quite destroyed to the extent of an inch by five-eighths at its posterior part. The bone beneath is deeply injected with blood, soft, and spongy. The edges of the cartilage around this ulcer present a worm-eaten appearance, particularly at its posterior part. The cartilage of the inner condyle presents, about three-fourths of an inch from its posterior border, three irregular ulcers, of small size, and scattered over a surface half an inch square. The portion of cartilage between these ulcers is thinned, and easily separated from the bone beneath, which is deeply injected with blood. At the upper and anterior edge of the femoral cartilage is an irregular ulcer, three-fourths of an inch long by half an inch wide, laying bare the subjacent bone. On the outer articulating surface of the tibia the cartilage is entirely destroyed, with the exception of a mere rim at its circumference, which also presents a worm-eaten appearance from the existence of minute ulcers. The place left by the loss of the cartilage is occupied by a pulpy, fleshy-looking, gelatinous mass. On the inner articulating surface of the tibia are twelve small ulcers, perforating the substance of the cartilage, and scattered over the inner half of its circumference. The centre of this cartilage, over a space of three-fourths by half an inch, is very much thinned, and easily separated from the bone beneath, which shines through it of a bluish-red appearance. At the anterior part of this cartilage are two ulcers, perforating its substance, and measuring one-fourth of an inch in their longest diameter. The bone beneath is highly vascular. For two and a half inches below the articulating surface of the tibia the cancellous tissue is soft, easily broken down, and evidently much diseased. The condyles of the femur are in a similar condition. At the posterior part, immediately below the head of the tibia, is an opening communicating with the medullary canal, which for some distance is occupied by a reddish-brown, soft, unctuous, and gritty mass. This, under the microscope, is seen to consist of bony debris, blood-discs, pus-corpuscles, and fat-cells, which may be regarded as the contents of an abscess of the head and medullary canal of the tibia. The upper third of the shaft of the tibia is injected, and of a bright rose colour, in patchy distribution. The os calcis is extremely soft, its tissue opened out, filled with oil, and crushed by the slightest pressure between the thumb and finger.

Sections of the diseased condyles of the femur and of the head of the tibia exhibit, under the microscope, the characteristic changes of this stage of tuberculosis, namely, occupation of the cancelli by tuberculous deposit, detachment more or less complete of the lining membrane of the cancelli, partial or complete disintegration of the cancellous walls, exostoses springing at various points from the latter, and occupation by tuberculous and osseous deposit of the lacunæ.

CASE VIII.—W. H., a female, aged 44 years, of nervo-bilious temperament, by occupation a silk-winder, had suffered for twelve months from tuberculosis of the lower end of the right tibia. She stated that the disease commenced without any known cause; that, at one time, the soft parts above the inner malleolus would be so painful, hot, and tender to the touch, as to render her unable to put the foot to the ground; and that, at other times, these symptoms were to a great extent in abeyance, which permitted her to walk, although lamely, a short distance to her usual employment. Some time after the commencement of the disease, pus formed over the inner ankle, and was discharged; and shortly afterwards, another collection of pus discharged itself immediately above the external malleolus. These openings continued when the case, twelve months after its commencement, came under my care. They were somewhat depressed below the general surface, had thickened, everted edges, were surrounded by an inflammatory halo, and discharged a thin, yellowish-looking, curdy pus, with now and then a slight admixture of blood. A probe, inserted into the inner opening, passed directly into the substance of the corresponding malleolus; whilst the outer opening had no direct communication with diseased bone. The synovial membrane of the ankle-joint, and the soft tissues superjacent to the latter, were thickened to the extent of producing considerable deviation from the healthy appearance. She had lost flesh, looked pale, had a small, soft, and feeble pulse; but otherwise her general health was not materially affected, except during occasional aggravations of the local disease, when considerable disturbance was manifested by the general system.

In the treatment, I cut down upon the inner malleolus, gouged away all the diseased bone, stuffed the wound with lint, and applied warm-water dressing. This mode of treatment, coupled with a generous diet, the use of cod-liver oil, and exercise upon crutches in the open air, commencing as soon as possible after the operation, healed the wounds in three months. Three years afterwards she remained well, could walk strongly, and felt no uneasiness in the previously affected parts; nevertheless the synovial membrane of the ankle-joint and the superjacent soft tissues remained in their thickened condition.

CASE IX.—J. K., a female of nervo-bilious temperament, at the age of 14 sprained her right ankle, and shortly afterwards again injured it. These injuries caused the joint to swell; but lameness did not supervene sufficiently to attract the attention of her parents until six months after the latter injury. A neighbouring surgeon was now consulted, who attended the case for the next twelve months, during which time pus formed, and was evacuated by the lancet. Two years from the time the disease attracted the attention of her parents I took charge of the case. There was now considerable enlargement of the soft parts around the ankle-joint, on the outer side of which a small fistulous opening, with hard, everted edges, existed. A probe, introduced into this opening, passed into the head of the astragalus, which was found to be diseased. There was no inflammatory blush around the opening, which was situated in the centre of a depressed portion of the skin, and from which a scanty quantity of sero-curdy looking pus escaped. Manipulation of the joint provoked a certain uneasiness, which amounted to pain on any attempt to stand or walk with the diseased limb. When at rest, with the foot elevated, the affected part was easy. In the early part of the disease the general health suffered, and the patient lost flesh, which she had not as yet regained. Her appearance was, therefore, pale and thin. The skin was cool, the pulse natural, the tongue moderately clean, the appetite regular, and the sleep but little disturbed. There was no thirst ; the bowels were torpid, and menstruation was irregular.

In the treatment, the foot and ankle were surrounded by a starched bandage, in which a sufficient opening was made opposite the sinus for the exit of pus. The foot was borne about an inch from the ground by a sling passing round the neck, the patient was put upon crutches, and exercise in the open air was enjoined. The bowels were at first regulated by alterative doses of mercury with the compound rhubarb pill, and she took regularly, three times a day, four grains of the iodide of potassium in an ounce of bitter infusion. A generous diet was ordered, together with half a pint of porter daily. By and by, the iodide of iron was substituted for the preparation of potash ; and this, in a short time, gave place to the cod-liver oil, which was exhibited for many months, in doses from two drachms at the commencement, to an ounce three times a day at the termination of the case. During the exhibition of the cod-liver oil, a grain of the sulphate of iron, one-fourth of a grain of aloes, a grain of the extract of henbane, and two grains of the extract of gentian, were given in the form of pill every night and morning. Under this treatment she slowly but steadily improved ; menstruation became regular, several small portions of dead bone separated and were removed from the sinus which led to their position, and, in a little more than two years from my first attention to the case, the wound healed. Three years and a half, however, elapsed from the assumption of crutches before the condition of the joint admitted of their being laid aside. Four years have already passed since this occurrence, and the cure remains complete. Her father, writing to me on the 5th of March 1859, says, with respect to this case, that the ankle-joint appears to be " quite sound "—that it is not now swollen—that the patient can use it pretty well, but not so freely as the other—that she can manage short distances without fatigue, but that a long walk even yet distresses the joint.

The indications of treatment which arise, in the above stage of tuberculosis of bone, have for their object :—

    I. To remove the diseased bone by manual operation, or to favour its separation.

    II. To favour the healing process by local and constitutional means, and to relieve urgent symptoms.

In fulfilling the former indication, it ought always to be borne in mind, that, before recovery can take place, those portions of diseased bone which have either lost their vitality, or retain this in a very small degree, *must* be separated from those which are not similarly affected. The first object, therefore, of the surgeon should be—to effect, with as little delay as possible, this separation, by the employment of those means which a full knowledge of the extent of the disease and of the particular features of the case may suggest. Now, it has been already shown, that the extent of the disease may vary from tuberculosis of a very small portion of a bone to the complete invasion of the latter. Hence, the treatment, as to the extent of manual interference, must also vary. When tuberculosis has invaded the whole of a short bone, or the entire extremity of a long bone, recovery cannot, after the manifestation of the ulcerative stage, take place with retention of the diseased bone. This, therefore, must be removed by operative procedure ; and, to accomplish this object, either excision or amputation will be necessary. The former operation, when by it the whole disease can be removed, is the one to be preferred ; and of its beneficial results many examples have of late occurred in the elbow, knee, and ankle. When, however, excision cannot compass the whole disease, so as to leave on recovery a useful limb, amputation of the latter above the seat of disease must be performed. This is especially necessary when, in tuberculosis of the head of the tibia, abscess of the medullary canal has occurred in the manner before described. When, however, to operate by excision or amputation, and when to attempt a recovery without, must be determined by a careful and complete exploration of the diseased bone and adjacent joint. There should neither be too great haste to perform these operations, where there is still a probability that, by milder measures, the bone may yet recover; nor too much delay in adopting them, where the conviction of their necessity exists.

When the tuberculosis of bone is of limited extent, there ought, as a general rule, to be no delay in cutting down upon the diseased part, and in removing it, provided this can be done without opening a joint. This treatment is rendered palpably necessary by the fact —that the cancelli of the diseased part are stuffed with tuberculous exudation—that their lining membrane is detached from its connections and destroyed—that the lacunæ and their canaliculi are more or less occupied by tuberculous and osseous deposit—and that the nutrition of the diseased bone is consequently at an end. Its separation from the living bone *must* therefore take place ; and this, where circumstances are favourable, is better effected at once by art than by the prolonged efforts of nature. In doing this, the rule—to gouge away the diseased bone until the latter bleeds from all points —is a good guide, as to the extent to which operative procedure should be carried. A limited tuberculosis thus treated, will frequently be followed by recovery, when, by non-interference, the disease would progress from little to more, and ultimately endanger the safety of the limb. This progression is, under such circumstances, due to the admission of air to the diseased bone, by which disintegration of the latter, and metamorphosis of the tuberculous exudation, are effected as before explained. It ought, therefore, to be an axiom in the treatment of this disease, to exclude air, as far as practicable, from contact with tuberculous bone. From this it follows, that abscesses connected with tuberculous bone should not, as a general rule, be opened; and that, where sinuses already exist, the diseased bone to which they lead, ought, when practicable, to be removed as soon as possible by operative procedure. Where the disease is too limited for excision or amputation—where its removal by the gouge is likewise impracticable, as is the case where tuberculosis affects that part of a bone which enters so fully as the head of the astragalus into the composition of a joint—and where, in consequence, the external air gains admission to the seat of disease through the cavity of the latter,—constitutional and local measures of position, and of a more gentle character than the above, are the only means to be adopted.

To favour the healing process, and thus to fulfil the second indieation of treatment in this disease, regard must be had to both local and constitutional measures. So long as the local symptoms are of an acute character, the affected part must be laid at perfect rest in a non-dependent position; and must likewise be soothed by occasional anodyne fomentations, and by the assiduous application of the warm-water dressing, or of a bread-sop poultice, which latter is, in many instances, productive of more benefit than the former remedy. At this stage the internal treatment should consist of an occasional mercurial alterative, together with anodynes, diaphoretics, diuretics, and occasional laxatives or mild aperients; whilst the diet should be of an unstimulating character. As soon, however, as the state of the affected part and the condition of the general system will admit of a tonic plan of treatment, this must be adopted without delay. With this view, the cod-liver oil, iodide of potassium in decoction of sarsaparilla or some vegetable infusion, the various preparations of iron in combination with vegetable bitters, together with a generous diet, and the cautious use of malt liquor or wine, will be prescribed with advantage.

An essential element, too, in the treatment at this point, is—active exercise in the open air. This ought *never* to be neglected when the patient is able to undertake it; nevertheless the affected part must not be used. To avoid this, slings, properly applied splints or bandages, and, in the case of the lower extremities, crutches, must be adopted. I am well persuaded that, were these means pursued to the extent which they deserve, a much greater success would attend the treatment of this disease than is at present the case. To confine the patient to bed when he is capable of leaving it—to torture him with setons, issues, or moxas, in the vain hope of curing the disease—and to allow a tuberculous bone to be used whilst the disease is yet progressing, are quite opposed to our views of the constitutional origin of tubercle, and to the pathological data which I have advanced. A free supply of oxygen is essential to the well-being of the body; motion of the latter, by accelerating the circulation and respiration, increases that supply; therefore, in tuberculosis, which requires the invigoration of the constitutional powers, exercise should be enjoined whenever it is not contra-indicated by other circumstances and conditions. Where, too, medicinal properties applicable to the constitutional treatment of the disease, exist either in the atmosphere or in the waters of a place, thither should the patient be removed as soon as practicable. Hence, the sea-coast for the former, and certain inland towns of England for the latter, reason, are the proper places of resort for such invalids.

By such means, then, as the above, timely applied and perseveringly carried out, we shall without delay, not only conduct the disease to the issue which its particular conditions indicate; but, by doing so, we shall frequently be the means of preserving lives, valuable in themselves, which would otherwise, by the continued ravages of the disease, be ultimately destroyed.